howard
&
charles
at the
factory

a short novel
by dave housley

Outpost19 | San Francisco
outpost19.com

Housley, Dave
Howard and Charles at the Factory / Dave
Housley

ISBN 978-1-944853-70-9 (pbk)
ISBN 978-1-944853-71-6 (ebk)

Library of Congress Control Number: 2019956238

Howard and Charles at the Factory by Dave Housley
is part of the ongoing Short-ish series of novellas
and extended essays, published by Outpost19.
Learn more at outpost19.com/Shortish.

OUTPOST19

ORIGINAL PROVOCATIVE READING
SAN FRANCISCO | @OUTPOST19

"We love Pittsburgh.
Thank you very much.
Wow, what a crowd, huh?
Just beautiful, thank you.
So nice, so nice.
We're going to bring back your coal industry,
your steel industry.
We're bringing it back.
Remember that,
we're bringing it back, folks."

Donald Trump Campaign Speech
April 13, 2016

End of the day, factory whistle cries
Men walk through these gates with death in their eyes
And you just better believe, boy
Somebody's gonna get hurt tonight
It's the working, the working, just the working life

Bruce Springsteen, "Factory"

howard
&
charles
at the
factory

1

HOWARD PARKS THE LINCOLN in the familiar spot. He takes a moment to savor this feeling, so long in coming. He looks at the factory in the distance, at his own grizzled hands on the wheel, and he feels it again, the swell of pride and relief and validation. And then, like so many days in the past, he puts sentiment behind him, swallows the emotion like a bite of meatloaf, and goes about his business. He picks up the Thermos and lunch bucket and his camp chair, and walks the familiar path. They have let the whole thing go to hell, of course: the sidewalk is cracked and broken and the lawn, always so carefully tended, is nothing more than a weedy field.

He is a little surprised that the new people in charge would have let it stay this way, but it is just the first day, and even the big man can't do everything, Howard supposes, when all is said and done. Just like he thought all along, they have made a real mess of things and it will take time to clean it all up.

He walks the broken sidewalk and turns the corner to the entrance and pauses at what he sees: Charles, here already and waiting in his own camp chair, sipping coffee and reading the Post-Gazette. He smiles. Of course. He wonders who else will show up today.

"Charles," he says, as he settles the camp chair and pours himself a cup of coffee.

"Thought I might see you here," Charles says. He nods and tips the coffee cup and hands over the sports page. "Penguins won again," he says. "Things are looking up."

"You can say that again," Howard says. He realizes he is nervous, the first time in years, but it's much better than the anger that had been swelling in his gut for the past decade or so, better than the boredom and the futility and the embarrassment. "You think they'll have us on the same jobs?" he says.

"I suppose it would be best to get us back to what we know," Charles says.

This makes sense. He was almost worried that they would be sitting at computers now, or that this would feel more like the job interviews he has shown up for and left before they started, cattle calls where they herded him into a room with fat teenagers and Mexicans and dead-eyed losers who were twenty years younger than him and looked like they had given up long ago. "Time is it?" he says.

Charles adjusts in his chair and checks his watch. Now he is remembering that Charles has his ways about him, a certain set of airs. "Eight," Charles said. "Should be starting up here soon."

"You think they…" Howard starts, and then he remembers everything that happened already. "Never mind," he says.

"Yeah, maybe because it's the first day," Charles says. "You done with that sports?"

Howard hands the section over and accepts the front page. "Thanks," he says. On the cover, a giant picture of a big man with his hand on the Bible, accepting his proper position. Howard looks around. It is a little weird that nobody else is here yet. It is somehow unnerving that the lawn has not been mowed. He puts it out of his mind. He can't possibly expect all the details of the transition to be worked out yet. He watches a jet sail over his head and away into the clear blue sky. He watches the trail left behind. He remembers something about those chemtrails, how they are really part of a weapons program or messages to the Soviets. Thankfully all of this nonsense will be over soon. Is over. He looks at his watch again. 8:15. Fifteen minutes late. This is not normal. He stands and tries to act casual. "I might…" he says, and takes a few steps toward the factory door.

"Locked," Charles says. Something about his tone is annoying, arrogant.

"Just thought I'd try," Howard says. "Guess I'm ready to get back to it."

"Hear you there, guy," Charles says. He crosses his legs. "Sure they'll be here soon. Maybe just…I don't know."

"Yeah, sure, definitely," Howard says. He sits back down in his chair and looks at the sky. The chemtrail is still there.

That is another one of the signs, he remembers: the chemtrails, they just stay there like graffiti in the goddamn beautiful blue American sky. Soon all of this will be over and the sky will be clear and clean again, the way he remembers it. He looks at the locked door, at their two cars sitting in the parking lot, all the empty spaces and the weeds and the broken sidewalk, at the dark windows of the factory behind them. "They'll definitely be here soon," he says. "Definitely."

2

HOWARD TAPS OUT a Bo Diddley beat with his foot, tap tap tap, tap-tap. Tap tap tap, tap-tap. He should have brought music, a book, the phone Leah gave him for Christmas a few years ago, before she moved and closed up on him and left a shell of a daughter in her place, a phone call on his birthday, on Christmas, every now and then a late-night text that seems more like a challenge, another test he has already failed without realizing he was being tested: I cannot believe you voted for that person.

He regards the factory in the distance. So many hours spent there, so many...when he thinks about it he can't really remember many specific things about the job. There was the day they had to shut down in the middle of a shift because of the Three Mile Island thing, some kind of rumors about the Russians and industrial targets. There was the time when Youndt lost the fingers, the splash of blood across his uniform and Old Snyder wiping down the line with spray oil and a towel from the break room. He remembers that Youndt never shouted, just yelped and grumbled goddamnit and wrapped the stumps in his handkerchief and walked out without another word. He remembers Charles looking over at Old Snyder and saying "lucky bastard will never work again" and then "workers' comp" when Old Snyder clearly didn't understand the implication.

Charles has always had his ways.

Nothing is happening at the factory. Nothing is happening in the woods. Charles just reads his newspaper.

Howard taps his feet: tap tap tap, tap-tap. Tap tap tap, tap-tap.

"Can you not?" Charles says. "Whatever you're doing."

Howard places his feet flat on the ground. "Sorry," he says. "It's just, I mean…"

The newspaper stays in place. Howard stands. Still nothing at the factory, still nothing in the woods. The wind whistles through the trees. In the distance, a motor starts. The sky is blue and cloudless, a perfect day. He watches a plane move across the horizon, leaving the grey smear of a chemtrail behind. There are chemicals in those trails, but also communications of some kind, messages being conveyed. He is not sure if the message is physical, like an old fashioned smoke signal, or if the trails are somehow made of messages, data, filled with bits or bytes or ions or ones and zeros. Data. There is data in everything now. As far as Howard knows that chemtrail might contain the entire sports section of the failing fake news New York Times. It could be where they are hiding her emails.

"You believe that?" he says.

Charles waits a beat. "Um-hmmm," he says, but Howard knows he is not agreeing so much as placating, patting him on the head, asking him to go into another room to play so the grown-ups can read their paper.

The chemtrail looks like a zipper, a cut, a wall dividing before and after, this place and that place. "You know about those, right?" he says.

"Um-hmmm" Charles says. The newspaper remains in place, a chemtrail of black ink and pulp between them.

Howard feels the urge return again like indigestion, an uncomfortable and unwelcome feeling brewing deep inside: it would be nice to talk to somebody. To just talk. Really talk. He remembers those moments before they would start, everybody waiting in line in their uniforms, having a last sip of coffee, a last drink from the water fountain, the smokers out in the parking lot getting one last one in before the shift. He remembers that Old Snyder always knew the bartenders in every bar, that Fisher always seemed to know everybody, that Zinn was always so generous but mostly, Howard suspected, because he wanted to get really drunk, that Korver would make a big show of buying the first round and then shrink into the wall for the rest of the night.

He has taken to going out to the Denny's for breakfast a few times a week, has almost succeeded in falling in with a group of State Farm agents who work the night shift, a group of okay-seeming guys in red golf shirts who talk about fantasy football and the Steelers and the Penguins and the shitty things their wives are doing, somebody named Sterling and what she wore to work that night, the changes that are coming or not. In Howard's day insurance men wore suits but the vein of conversation is familiar to him and although they are younger they treat him with what he will take as respect when he tries to tap himself in to the conversation.

Last week the main one, the one with Jake stitched on the sleeve of his golf shirt, even asked Howard a question: where did you work? He said. When Howard mentioned the factory they all shouted right or yes and threw up their hands and looked at the one with the glasses and the long beard like an argument had been settled.

He wracks his brain for things he can talk to Charles about. The factory? The Steelers? Restaurants? Weather? What do people talk about, anyway? He remembers having things to talk about, never feeling like he had to struggle, to think, to make up lists. When Leah was younger she would ask question after question and he was always so pleased to answer, or to take her to the library to look something up. He was a good father, a good provider. The factory was a good job. Now…well, now that they have corrected course, all of these things should be better again. Great again. It really was great, he thinks, Leah on his lap asking about cats or the sky or how cars work, taking off his gloves at the end of a long day, clapping Fisher or Zinn or Old Snyder on the back and asking where they were they going to have a few tonight.

He could talk to Charles about their children but eventually he would have to admit that he has not talked to Leah since the election. He could talk to Charles about the State Farm guys and the way they don't even wear suits to work anymore, even insurance men. He wonders if Charles knows any insurance men. Probably Charles still knows insurance men who do dress in suits, fancy white-haired insurance men who would like to tell you about this annuity or that fund. He could talk to Charles about fishing but he has not been fishing in years, not even with all of that time stretched out before him every day. He could talk to Charles about the Steelers but that coach they have now is just…not the kind of man to be coaching the Steelers.

"You believe that guy, the coach, that, what's his name?"

"What did Tomlin do now?" Charles says. He lowers the newspaper. His readers are drooped down on his nose and his eyebrow hairs are starting to shoot off in directions.

"Just…you know."

"Not the kind of man ought to be coaching at that level," Charles says.

"What I say. It's just different."

"Expect it won't be long now for him," Charles says.

7

He brings the newspaper back to his face and the divider is up again. Howard looks to the sky. The chemtrail is just a faint line, the blue slowly stitching itself back together. He wonders if whatever information it is supposed to have delivered has been received. He wonders if the big man has found a way around this one yet, or if he is now the one on the receiving end. There will be much that he will have to get used to, to find out, even a titan of industry like him, so rich and New York smart. Of course they would not have gotten to the factory yet. The factory is on a list but so are so many other things. Those people have been so reckless with the country, like the country is a house that was taken over by hippies so of course when the right men are back in charge, they are going to have to spend a good deal of time cleaning out all the hippie stuff, the Mexican stuff and the black stuff and the gay stuff and the swamp stuff that Howard doesn't even know what it is but the big man does. The big man knows about all of it and he is the only one who can clean it up again.

He could talk to Charles about the big man but he is worried Charles knows more about him than Howard and then he would just wind up feeling small again, out of the loop, not good enough. He stands, checks the factory. Nothing happening. He sits back down. They will get to the factory. They will need to clean up some other things but they will get to the factory in due time and Howard will be right here when they do.

3

HOWARD WAKES UP In the chair. He checks his watch. Six forty-five. His hands are numb and his knee is starting to hurt. The parking lot is empty, the sky concrete gray, just beginning to yellow around the edges. In the distance, he sees Charles relieving himself in the field near the woods. They have settled on a spot for that and it seems like a kind of decision, an affirmation.

He stands and stretches, does a few jumping jacks. When Ginny was still alive they were going to the Silver Sneakers at the Y. She even had him doing a yoga class once a week. The teacher was young, in her forties, and Howard liked the way she walked around, the way she talked, the tight black pants she would wear to talk them through the stretches and the end part where they were just laying there. He used to call it advanced stretching and Ginny would laugh and fill up the water bottle, pat him on the arm and then gather the keys to the Lincoln.

He wonders what the rest of them would think about that. Howard at yoga. He is going to get a ribbing if he ever tells them the story. Charles is walking back now, a slight limp in his left leg. The days on the line, the months and years have cost them all something. Youndt his fingers. Fisher his back. Charles and Howard their knees. He wonders if they will have longer breaks now but then puts the idea out of his mind. It is a Democrat idea. A liberal notion. Socialist. It was his right to give the knee and he gave it, one shift at a time.

Charles sits down and picks up the newspaper.

"Morning," he says.

"Morning," Howard says. "I think I'm going to…"

"Do what you have to do," Charles says, and Howard can't tell if he is making a joke or commentary. It was always so hard to figure out where Charles was coming from. It would be better if it was Youndt or Fisher or Old Snyder here with him. They will probably show up soon. Maybe this morning. He checks his watch. An hour until starting time. The parking lot is empty but then again none of them used to show up early, now that he thinks about it. Now that he thinks about it he remembers getting in at 7:50 every day. Wake up at seven, drink your coffee, read the sports, head out to the factory.

"What have you been doing, you know, since," he says.

"I don't know that that's--what's the word--relevant," Charles says. He always did have his ways about him.

"Okay yep," Howard says. "I'm just going to…"

"Do what you have to do," Charles says.

Howard limps toward the field. He unzips, makes sure he is facing away from Charles. The forest is beautiful but he knows what it is like in there. He remembers hunting with his father, wading through brush and trees, bugs and stickers and weeds to find their tree stand, sitting there and watching, struggling to stay awake, eating Payday bars and just waiting for some poor deer to walk into their vision and his father would put a hand on his arm, strong. He would nod and raise the gun.

He finishes and waits a moment. He tries to think of something to talk to Charles about. The Steelers are done playing. The Penguins are good again. Should they go find a new newspaper, a hot coffee, a McMuffin with sausage and hash browns? But what would happen if they came back to find a line of men in their place, a parking lot full of Fords and Chevys, the factory churning back to life without them?

There is a ripple in the forest, something moving. He expects a deer and turns to Charles, waves a hand, but the man is just sitting there, reading his newspaper. Something pokes its head through the trees and Howard steps back. He steps back again. It can't be but it is, standing there at the forest's edge, it's green head poking out, is what looks like a dinosaur. A T-rex? It is as tall as he is, a few feet taller, standing upright, a lizard head covered with sparse feathers, an alert look about it, legs like tree trunks, a tail that disturbs the brush as it twitches slowly behind. A dinosaur.

He turns to Charles but he is just reading his paper. Charles would...Charles has his ways. Charles would never understand. What if this isn't real? Is he losing his mind? What if they have to interview for their jobs again and Charles tells them Howard has been talking about dinosaurs in the woods.

The creature looks at him. It almost seems to be smiling. He is not sure why but he is overcome with emotion--and it has been such a long time. The factory closing down and then Ginny and then Leah off to San Francisco. San Francisco. But that is all over now. The animal is moving up and down, back and forth. It looks right at him. Should he be afraid? Should he make himself big, make noise, shout and stomp?

The animal makes a sound. Cheep cheep. It raises to its full height. Howard backs up a step, then another. Is this real? His heart is racing but he is not afraid and wonders briefly why that might be. The animal takes a step forward. Cheep cheep. They lock eyes and Howard flashes on something familiar, a warm feeling, and old one from better and simpler times. And then with a quick burst the creature turns and slips through the trees and it is gone. Gone. Howard looks back at Charles. He checks the forest again. The sky is clear blue, not a chemtrail in sight. It is seven fifteen. Today may be the day. A dinosaur? He will need to keep this to himself. He will need to not mention the yoga or the dinosaur or Leah in San Francisco if they have to interview for their jobs again. He remembers the interview at Home Depot, the manager kept checking his phone and laughing and then not explaining what was so funny. "What's that, what's so funny?" Howard had asked.

"I think we're done here thanks!" the guy said. He was Indian, or Iraqi, Palestinian, one of those, one of the ones with the dark skin who talks just like everybody else. "Thanks so much," he said as he looked at his phone again. "We'll be in touch one way or another."

4

HOWARD WAKES UP and notes that the pain in his stomach has gone away. This is a good thing and not a good thing. He stands and regards the factory in the distance. Is that a light on? He listens, watches. He should wake up Charles. He should comb his hair, put on a clean set of clothes. What he would really like is a stack of pancakes and the Denny's three egg special. Bacon and home fries and a nice Coca Cola.

He bends. The ache in his knee is no worse. That is something. He stands upright, puts his arms out to his sides, reaches for the sky the way they told him to in Silver Sneakers. He flashes on that yoga instructor, then on Ginny with her glasses pushed up on her head, her sweatpants and the sweat-wicking shirt she had bought just for the Silver Sneakers. Twelve years, six months, forty...three days? Forty-five days? Is he losing track of the days out here?

He watches the factory. More lights will be coming on soon, first in the executive area and then on the floor. The outside lights should be on, though, the whistle should have sounded once already. There are no cars in the parking lot, no sounds of engines coming from the road.

The lighted room goes slowly dark and the sun peaks over the factory roof.

He breathes in and out. In and out. In. Out. He pushes his hands up over his head. What did the yoga lady used to say? Reach for the sun. He always thought it was somehow significant, a personality indicator at least, that she used to say reach for the sun even though reach for the stars was sitting right there, the flip side of the coin. He is the kind of person who notices things like that, the way the State Farm guys wait until the main one has ordered and then order something like what he favors -- some days an omelette, some days an all-American breakfast, some days a breakfast sandwich or a burrito or pancakes. He notices the way Charles flips his newspaper in front of his face when he sees Howard coming back from one of his little walks, the way Charles always addresses him as if he is some kind of inferior, an employee or a student or a child.

Howard reaches for the sun. He places his hands on his hips and leans to the right to stretch his...what kind of muscle is it that he is stretching? He remembers the yoga instructor, the slight swell of her breasts as she leaned over, the calm in her voice even though she was practically shouting, and he is teetering, teetering, grabbing at the camp chair and then falling and then he is on the ground, pain in his shoulder, in his knee. He rolls over onto his back. He remembers when Albright's knee gave out and he hit his head on the conveyor and Mr. Tom Williams himself drove him to the hospital, kept him talking all the time so he wouldn't pass out, slip into a coma or worse.

"The hell now?" Charles says. He stirs in his camp chair, finally spots Howard where he lays on the ground, face up, camp chair sprawled across his belly. "What the sam hill?"

"Was trying to...limber up a little," Howard says. He sits up, takes an inventory of the shoulder, the knee. There is a sharp pain in his ankle that he doesn't think was there before, a little pain starting up in his thumb. "I thought I saw the...I thought they were..."

"He thought he thought," Charles says, struggling to get out of the camp chair. He regards Howard there on his back. "He thought so much had a great fall."

Howard pushes the chair off his stomach. He flexes his thumb, feels the shoulder again. Hopefully there is nothing broken. Hopefully he will not find later that he hasn't broken some other bone, something he can't even feel right now.

Charles reaches out a hand and Howard accepts it. He stands, straightens the camp chair. There is nothing happening in the factory.

"Are you hungry?" he says.

Charles pulls something out of his jacket and hands it across the space between them. A Powerbar. Chocolate.

"I...have you..." Howard starts.

Charles points to his little Civic sitting in the parking lot. "In the trunk," he says.

Howard just sits, stunned. He unwraps the bar. He has never seen anything so beautiful as the waxy chocolate coating. Just then a rumble and music, tires moving fast on the factory road.

They share a look and wait. Could this be the trucks that will carry the supplies needed to make the factory great again? Would they start by repairing the road? The factory itself? Or would they just turn the lights on again and start up like nothing ever happened?

The big man likes building things, tall things, important things like skyscrapers and football leagues and mail order steak companies. He is a builder. Maybe they will knock the factory down and build a new one, a beautiful new skyscraper factory right here in the grave of the old one.

"Hey," Charles says, just as a truck appears on the road. Or is it a truck? It is like a truck in a cartoon, a movie truck, a truck that has eaten some other trucks and grown accordingly. It is silver, with massive wheels, a loud grinding engine. In the bed, attached to the cab, an overgrown exhaust pipe pushes black smoke up into the air. The windows are tinted. It pulls in and pauses. The window rolls down to reveal a young man. He is early Twenties, maybe younger, with hair shaved close on the sides and swooping up over his head in a spectacular pompadour. He looks at Howard and Charles. He nods, and the window goes up again. The truck does a slow three point turn. The license plate reads USABRAD. Howard can see a confederate flag hanging in the back window. A white outlined sticker of some cartoon character urinating on something is plastered on the top right corner of the window.

"What the…" Howard says.

"Quite the truck," Charles says.

The truck spins wheels and rocks fly across the parking lot. Smoke belches up into the sky, thick and black.

"Was that…do you think…"

"Just some kid," Charles says. "Probably looking for a place to take his girl this weekend or something."

Howard stares at the trail of smoke leading back toward the road, toward the city, his apartment and the Dennys and the YMCA and the other places where he and Ginny once made their life, unremarkable moment by unremarkable moment. That boy was younger than Leah, in his twenties, old enough to afford tires that must cost…Howard has no idea how much tires like that would cost. He regards his Lincoln in the far parking lot where it has been standing for…how many days now? Weeks? A month? The check engine light has been on for almost a year but that is all computers now, just another way for them to get you worried and then take some of your money, some young Mexican puts a machine up to the machine in your car and the light goes out and they send you to the girl at the desk to pay them for the pleasure.

"Not any more," he says, and only realizes just as the words are coming out of his mouth that he's saying them out loud.

"Galldarn right," Charles says.

Howard turns to look at Charles but he is sitting back down, picking up his newspaper. Howard watches the smoke trail fade into the sky. Above him, all is blue. No truck smoke or chemtrails or even clouds today, just the pale slice of the sun moving ever skyward. He wonders what that cartoon could possibly have been, some character urinating on another. When did they start putting this type of thing on their cars?

"Well," Charles says, snapping his newspaper and settling into the camp chair. "Suppose we best get back to it."

5

HOWARD HAS DEVELOPED a cough. He hocks a disturbingly hard ball of phlegm, noting that over the past few days the color has turned from white to yellow to brown.

"Bless you," Charles says from behind his newspaper. This started as a joke but now it feels like a complaint, a commentary Charles is making on Howard and his cough, the fact that he's been spitting increasingly worrisome things out of his mouth for the past however many days.

Howard stands up and sits down. He should have brought something to read. He stopped even asking Charles about the newspaper days ago. At this point, the newspaper and the front page picture of Donald with his hand on the good book is as much a part of the landscape as the broken sidewalk and weedy field and the forest behind it, as much as the factory itself, still dark and shuttered.

"I'm just gonna…" Howard says, nodding at the field.

"Do what you have to do," Charles says from behind his paper.

Howard walks gingerly toward the place where they have been relieving themselves. His bad knee aches and he longs to take off his shoes, but he has a feeling that if he takes them off he may never be able to get them back on again. He has lost track of the days other than he has been coughing now for four and the hole showed up in his glove three days ago. It has been long enough, he knows, that the men who are going to open the factory back up again should have been here by now.

He thinks on this again. It is possible this means the big man himself will be the one to open up. That would explain the delay, at least. He would like to talk to Charles about this but Charles has made it clear he is not open to this discussion. On the third day, Howard tried all the doors and walked the circumference to be sure they hadn't established a new entrance somewhere else. He cleaned the smudged windows and looked in and saw the garbage and the rats and the dirt and no indication that anybody was getting anything ready, and Charles just sat there with his newspaper, every now and then shaking his head or pursing his lips in his way.

"Happy?" he said, when Howard finally gave up and sat down in his lawn chair again.

"No," Howard said. They haven't spoken of it since.

Now Howard relieves himself in the spot they has been using for this purpose. He looks into the woods for any signs of the animal he saw on the second day. As usual, nothing. He zips up, turns back toward the factory, and is shocked to see a car heading his way. He is momentarily embarrassed to be seen so obviously finishing up his business, especially by the head men, but then he remembers how pleased they are going to be to see them back here, him and Charles, ready and willing to go back to work. His heart beats faster and the emotion wells in his throat. They are here. Finally.

He walks as fast as he can back to the factory entrance, watching the gravelly road. It is some kind of official vehicle, municipal, so maybe not the men in charge but maybe the men who come before them, the ones who need to approve the re-opening. A slight doubt smudges his emotion: the big man said they weren't going to need things like approvals anymore, government bureaucrats screwing everything up with their regulations and handouts and neutral bathrooms and climate change websites. But it has only been…how long now? Even the big man can't do everything right away. He limps back to Charles, standing now and smiling.

"Well," Howard says.

"That's right," Charles says. He leans over and shakes Howard's hand. They lock eyes for a moment. Howard flashes on his father, heading out the door, lunchpail in hand, heading to the very factory that stands shuttered behind them right now, the one that will soon open up again. Howard allows himself the brief indulgence before it is time to get back to work: his father would be proud.

Howard hears a car door and something changes in Charles' face. He turns and sees two men, dressed for outside work and younger than he would have expected, standing outside the vehicle. One of them has a long beard like a prospector, or the kid who makes the coffee in the fancy coffee store Leah used to drag him to, before she moved to San Francisco. The other one is dark skinned and heavyset. Some kind of Mexican, Howard guesses. They open the trunk and bring out surveying equipment. They nod to Howard and Charles and talk to one another briefly, making some kind of joke. They spread a map on the hood of the car and the Mexican looks at something on his phone and then points to the map, then to a spot in the field.

Howard watches as the Mexican directs the bearded fellow to set up his equipment in a particular area. They are taking measurements, pecking away at one of those ridiculous computers everybody carries around all the time now. Charles is reading the newspaper again like nothing ever happened. Howard is still standing. He coughs, spits a ball of phlegm roughly the color and shape of a Hershey's kiss onto the crumbling sidewalk.

"Bless you," Charles says.

The men are moving casually but efficiently. The sun has started to set and Howard can feel in his bones how cold it is going to be tonight.

"Don't you…" he says. His voice is shaking and he stops before he betrays the emotion. Charles just reads his paper. Howard breathes deeply, in and out, in and out. The men go about their business in the field. "Maybe they're building a new factory," he says.

"That's the spirit," Charles says. He turns the page on his paper. "More like it at least."

Howard regards the front of the newspaper. Charles is right. Things will be great again. They have put the right man in charge, finally. "I'm going to just…" Howard says.

Charles turns a page. "Do what you have to do," he says, not even trying to hide the judgment.

Howard starts toward the men. His knee aches more than ever. He wonders how long it will take the rebuild the factory. He is embarrassed that he even imagined the old one would be good enough for the big man, with his gold and his money and his skyscrapers, his beautiful daughter and handsome sons, hotels and mail order steaks and reality television shows. Of course he would build a new factory, a fantastic factory, so much better than the old one. Can they build a skyscraper factory? Would they use real gold? He wonders if there will be a cafeteria in the new factory, or one of those coffee places. Maybe one of the machines with the little coffee pods. Maybe one for each and every one of them.

The men see him coming and pause in their work,

quizzical looks on their faces. Howard raises a hand. Behind them, he sees movement. The T-rex animal pokes its head out from behind a tree and regards the workers. It looks to Howard and their eyes lock. Go back, Howard thinks. He has been waiting to see the T-rex, scanning the forest, wondering if he was crazy, and now that it is back he knows instinctively that it must retreat into the forest, that whatever these men are doing will not be good for the dinosaur. He is surprised by the reaction, a deep well of emotion, a protective instinct he hasn't felt since Leah was young.

He can see it clearly now, the face narrower than the dinosaurs in the movies, covered in feathers. He realizes it is not a T-rex. It is too small, too feathery, too friendly to be a Tyrannosaurus. It blinks. He can see its chest moving up and down with each breath. Is it nervous? Excited? Does it...like him? The animal reminds him of a dog they had got for Leah when she was in middle school, a short-haired mutt with erect ears and a busy way about her. The animal moves up and down, like it is jogging in place. He will call it Mavis, after the dog.

"You having a tailgate over there?" the Mexican says, and Howard jumps. He turns to the man, younger than he had expected, just like everybody else. He is fat, wearing shorts and black socks with some kind of basketball sneaker. His accent is Pittsburgh.

"Tailgating?" Howard says.

"The beach chairs," the Mexican says. "You know Pitt ain't played a football game in a few months, man."

Howard nods. "Right," he says. "We're just... actually it's..." He pauses. Actually the factory and their jobs and the big man making everything great again is none of the Mexican's business. None of his business at all. None of those people's business, any of them. That

22

time is over and soon they will be back to football players standing for the pledge of allegiance, to closed borders and open factories filled with hard-working men like he and Charles, to yes sir and no ma'am and hot dogs and apple pie and clear blue skies.

"So…" he says. He looks to the animal, still running in place. He wonders if he can casually throw a rock toward the forest, scare the creature back into the brush. He bends down and pretends to be tying his shoe. When he stands back up again, the dinosaur has disappeared. "So," he says, "what you fellas doing out here?"

He reaches his hand out to shake and the bearded fellow returns the gesture. He is young, in his twenties, with a ring in his nose and the same large glasses Howard remembers the coffee maker wearing. Howard nods to the Mexican and the man nods back, a quizzical look on his face.

"So how long you think it'll be?" he asks.

"How long?" the Mexican says. "For what? To get the wells up?"

"The factory," Howard says. "I mean, I'm sure it'll be better, you know he doesn't stand for anything but the best, but we were hoping…" He sees something changing on the Mexican's face.

"This is all going to be pumps," he says, his voice soft, his accent more pronounced now. Local Pittsburgh. "Natural gas." He glances at the bearded man and they share a look. "Well, we better…" he starts.

"Right. Right," Howard says. He scans the forest, relieved at least that the animal has retreated for now. "I'll leave you to it." He turns and sees Charles still sitting in his chair, still reading his newspaper. Even from this distance, he looks determined, resolute. So the men are not here to build a new factory. So they will work in the old one. So the big man has some other things to worry about first, like natural gas.

Howard bends his knee and feels the ache. His finger is numb where the hole has opened up in his glove. The men are putting their equipment back in the car. They beep and wave and then Howard is watching the tail lights retreat along the broken road. Charles just reads his newspaper. Howard sits back down and waits.

6

HOWARD STANDS WHEN he hears the cars. His knee aches. He coughs, spits, wipes his mouth. His hand comes back streaked with blood. He checks the factory. Over the past few days he has developed a fear that something will start up without them, that they will wake up one morning to find a line of men standing on the other side of the factory, or coming out after a shift, or that they will be awakened by the whistle calling the end to one shift and the beginning of another.

They have gotten used to the occasional car, almost always somebody turning around with an embarrassed wave at the two men and their camp chairs, but this is more than just one car. Charles moves his newspaper aside and raises his eyebrows. "What's this then?" he says.

"Cars. Plural," Howard says.

What would a motorcade sound like? Something like this, several vehicles moving at a cautious but sure pace. He wonders what he would say, would it be better to make a joke – well it took you long enough but I'm ready to get back to it – or just shake the big man's hand and keep his mouth shut. The big man likes people who like him. He likes people who bring something to the table. He likes veterans, football players, Playboy bunnies and businessmen and princes and television show hosts. Howard is pretty sure they are going to hit it off.

He looks for the vehicles. It would be a line of SUVs and then a limo, he supposes. The big man does like his limos, if the newspaper is to be believed. But no, they are not to be believed. Fake news. It is all such a relief, to be done with all of it. He had been growing suspicious of the newspaper and the radio and the television for quite some time, always with their science and facts and diversity. Even the pretty weathergirl on the "coverage you can count on" is some kind of Mexican or Iraqi now. And he is supposed to believe that she knows something he doesn't, some Iraqi fake boob teenager from who knows where?

He wonders what happened to the last one, the nice brunette who looked a little like Ginny when she was younger. They are all being moved aside, shunted, replaced by these Mexicans and Pakistanis and kids with things in their noses and neck tattoos, staring at their phones and not even telling what it is that's so goddamn funny in there.

It is not a motorcade. It is four trucks and a few sedans, all of them white with a green logo that says "Northwest Appalachian Energy." They park along the field.

"Don't think that's our party," Charles says, picking up the newspaper. Howard wishes again that it was Youndt or Fisher or Old Snyder. Charles has always had his ways.

The Mexican and the guy with the beard get out of the first car and begin pulling equipment out of the trunk. They place several things that look like suitcases on the ground. They are heavy and each of them carries one side. They work with caution. The Mexican is wearing shorts and black socks again. The bearded guy has arms full of tattoos and Howard guesses this is one of those bearded fellows who Leah would refer to as a hip something. Not a hippie. A hipster. Something about him just seems a little self-satisfied, a little too prepared.

Howard is sure that the young man was not pleased with the results of the election.

"What do you think they're…" he says.

"I suppose something to do with energy," Charles says. Howard does not like his snippy tone. If Youndt was here they would probably have a cabin built already, a tent at least. If Fisher was here they'd have some kind of card game going, probably ten more fellows out here with them. Fisher always did manage to draw a crowd.

"Suppose so," Howard says, in a tone that he hopes Charles takes as snippy.

Howard does not like the looks of the men in the trucks, a ragged, dirty collection of Mexicans and people who look like they have been sleeping in bus stations, mottled beards and squinty eyes and dirty shirts and tattoos.

"What the…" he says.

Charles puts down the paper. "Typical bunch of ingrates, am I right?"

Howard sits back down. He is stunned, unsure of what to do. "You're not wrong," he says. He stands back up. Should he go over there and say something? But who would he say it to when the one who seems to be in charge is a Mexican himself. He could try to pull the hipster aside and talk to him, man to man, but he has a feeling that approach would not work either. Best to bring it up, maybe, with the head men in charge of the factory. For now he will watch. He will make notes, make himself useful. When the right men get here, the ones who are really in charge, he will be ready.

7

THEY TAKE BREAKS every hour. One break every hour. He can see the Mexican in the shorts start to look at his watch -- look look look okay fellas, break. When Howard and Charles worked at the factory they had a morning break, a lunch break, an afternoon break. Fifteen minutes half an hour ten minutes. Just enough time to visit the bathroom or have a smoke or a Mr. Pibb or a Tastykake. These people sprawl all over the ground. They lay down, sit on the grass, wander the perimeter, each one of them looking at their phones like Terry Bradshaw was in there telling them the secret of life.

"No way to live," Charles says, nodding at them now on their three o' clock break. "Looking at those things all the time. These kids. These millenials, they just…" he shakes his head, leaves it at that, and for once Howard is pleased to be on the same wavelength as Charles and his airs. Neither one of them has to say another word.

The big man does love his Twitter of course. Howard almost wishes he had tracked down the phone that Leah had given him. What did she call it? A burner. He has no idea what that means other than he had been given something less, had less assumed of him, been placed on the bench before he even had a chance to show what he could do. He is relatively sure they will be forbidden in the new factory, like so many of the new things should be. How many fingers would Youndt have left if he had been fiddling with his Twitter all day while…he can't quite remember what it is that they did, but he knows it was good, important, that they worked hard and got respect.

The Mexican and his charges have been spray painting things on the ground, looking at machines, moving other machines around and then talking to people on the phone. They have created a grid, a massive hashtag of chemtrail graffiti right there on the beautiful green grass, not fifty yards from where Mavis roams the wood's edges. These people should be landscaping, weeding, pulling strawberries in the desert heat somewhere in California or Venezuela and they are spray painting some mysterious pattern next to the factory parking lot of all places. It is strange that the men in charge have not come yet, but these much lesser men – could he even call them men? -- these others have come first. Howard realizes with a jolt that it is all part of the plan. He is part of the plan. He and Charles are here. They have stationed themselves at the factory. They are hard-working American men and they can be relied upon to carry out a job without being asked twice, without any handouts or yoga mats or handheld personal computing devices or water breaks. They have been tasked with a job and Howard is darn sure going to do it.

8

HOWARD TAKES THE route he thinks of as Factory Right. He has taken to going on little walks, "excursions" is what Charles calls them, around the factory one way, around the other way, along the road between the factory and the field, the place that he thinks of as The Border, a name even more appropriate with the proliferation of Mexicans working for Northwest Appalachian Energy. When they are gone he walks the treeline, looking for signs of Mavis. Yesterday he found footprints, bird-like and the size of a volleyball, and trailed them into the forest until he could almost not see the field, the rocky driveway, the factory in the distance, Charles no doubt sitting steadfast and judgmental in his camp chair.

But there must be rules. Without rules there would be chaos and he knows this, knows it all the more now, after that man and his eight years of giveaways and open borders and poor children being molested in pizza ping pong parlors. Without rules they would be right back where they were before and it is up to men like Howard, like Charles and the big man and Wells Fargo and strong Russians who ride horses shirtless to make the rules, and so he has made one: if you can see the factory, you are still at the factory, still in line, still among the chosen when the men in charge arrive to turn the lights back on. So even though he has allowed himself the indulgence of imagining all that might flow from her discovery, he retraced his steps until he was again standing in the field, among the strange tools of the Mexicans and the bearded hipster, staring into the darkening forest making the sound he remembers Mavis making: cheep cheep, cheep-cheep.

Now he walks Factory Right, wending in the dusty alley between the factory and the cracked executive parking area. None other than Mr. Tom Williams, the head man in charge, used to park his pick-up truck in the spot closest to the factory, furthest from the road. Howard can picture him – tall, salt-and-pepper hair, thick like the linebacker he was at Pitt. Mr. Williams bought himself a new truck every year. Ford F-150s. That was when America was great again – Fords and factories and Mr. Tom Williams stepping out of a brand new truck with a briefcase and a hard-hat, nodding to the fellows as they streamed in for the first shift.

Howard has been trying to take advantage of these forays. He is watching. He is noticing things: the shoe near the entrance to the factory, the place where somebody has written Gracie + Frank in white paint on the side of the factory wall, the lights on the distant hill that come on every night at seven forty-five. He wonders if they are automatic lights or a person like himself, a person who is home every day, regular, reliable, prone to habit, a person who might wait until seven forty-five every day, marking time, watching the news, checking the machine to make sure nobody has left any messages, watching and then confirming the time and then walking to the door and simply doing his job. Flick. Lights. 7:45. America needs rules. It needs lights. It needs hard-working American men to turn them on.

He wonders at how fast it all changed. The world was filled with men like himself and the light turner, men who watched and waited and did their jobs, did them like their fathers before them, quietly but firmly, without expectations or hand-outs. And then all of the sudden they were thrust into this new world, gender-neutral bathrooms and Mexicans in shorts spray-painting the green fields, chemtrails pushing information to the Russians or the Democrats right there in the clear blue sky. Right here, in Pittsburgh. Right up there. Right now.

He rounds the corner and notes the tree that seems to be growing strangely, the branches close to the factory are stunted and broken, the branches on the other side grown out and up, dragging the entire tree in what he imagines is a slow motion takedown. Could there be something, what is the word, environmental about the factory and the tree? It is certainly strange. He wonders what kind of tree it is. He never did learn the names of the trees and the flowers and the plants and he has been none the worse for it. The environment is definitely a Democrat issue and the big man is about making money, making money that will make them all great again. The big man would probably knock this tree, any tree, the entire forest near the Mexican project down in a huff if he could. He decides that he will not report anything about the strange tree when the new men in charge show up.

It is getting darker, the night settling in all around him as he walks. His knee stopped hurting a few days ago and he wonders if this is a bad or a good sign. He will chalk it up as a good thing, as a fitness thing, all of this walking, all of this noticing is doing his body good.

He hears a whirr and stops. He has taken to cataloguing the sounds at night – the insects buzzing, animals scurrying, Charles and his wet cough. But this is a new sound, a machine sound. He backs up until he is leaning against the brick factory wall. He pushes into the wall and it feels lightly warm, like a sleeping thing. Up in the sky, lights. A ship. A UFO, a long grey zeppelin just hanging there, little projectiles whirring, some kind of lights displaying a pattern that is not written in any language he has ever seen. It moves slowly and then stops. A light turns on, a search light, and it strafes the strange tree.

Howard wants to shout, to call out to Charles but something keeps him there against the wall of the factory, heart beating, something pushing at his throat like he wants to cry. He flashes on all of those movies but this is nothing like any of them. Will he be abducted? Will he be famous? Will this get the big man and the head men in charge out to the factory? Could this be the big man himself? He does like to make an entrance.

The machine is gigantic, half the size of a football field. It is beat up, like a warship, strafed with dings and dents and scratches, covered in smaller machines that rotate and whirr and expand and contract, like a giant insect that is covered with other insects, each of them whirring and winding to their own internal logic.

Howard holds his breath and watches the machine soar out of his view, over the factory. He walks carefully, slowly, to the other side of the strange tree and he hides there and watches as the UFO soars up and then pauses over the factory. The searchlight comes back on and Howard wishes that he had a camera so he could take a picture of this amazing machine blessing the factory, choosing it, smudging it like Father Castelucci on Ash Wednesday. He knew the factory was special. He knew that it would be special again.

His fingers are shaking, his heart beats wildly, the blood shoots through his veins. His vision is going shaky. He wonders if he is having a heart attack, a stroke. He finds himself sitting, then laying down. The hum feels like it is coming from inside his head, like he is inside the vehicle. For the first time he understands why people would want to be abducted, conveyed into another world.

He wants to share this with someone, Charles or Leah or Mr. Tom Williams himself. But it is Howard who has been chosen, who has been watching, who has been here all along waiting to get back to work and make it great again. He deserves this.

The UFO swirls the searchlight around the factory roof and then the whirr moves into a new register, deeper and higher at the same time. Howard wants to stand, to signal, to say I'm here, but his arms are frozen, his legs like noodles. He forces himself to relax, watch, notice.

There is no way Charles is not seeing this, hearing it at least, on the other side of the factory. The searchlight turns off and everything goes still for a moment and then a boom and the machine explodes up, almost as if the light is a catapult that shoots the UFO back up into space. It is there and then the light goes off and it is gone.

His hands are still shaking, the blood pumping through his system. He is sweating despite the chill in the night air. He sits up, shakes his hands, which have gone numb. He breathes. In and out. In and out. It was beautiful. The factory has been chosen. He stands, stretches, still staring at the place where the machine disappeared.

He rounds the corner, practically running. He feels like he is eighteen again, like he is new and clean and anything can happen. "Did you see it?" he shouts as soon as Charles comes into view.

But something is wrong. Charles is not standing, staring at the sky, not running toward him or hiding or clenching his fists in victory or amazement or even fear. Charles is sitting in his camp chair, reading his newspaper. "Did you…" Howard starts. His words come out expectant, exultant, his voice rough and excited.

Something tells him to tamp it down, that showing this hand is not in his best interest. "Did you see anything strange?" he says.

Charles keeps on reading. Finally he lowers the paper. "Strange?" he says.

Howard tries to read his face but as always there is nothing there but a mild layer of contempt. Charles has his ways about him. Howard looks to the sky again and Charles follows.

"Nice night," Charles says.

Howard lets it sit between them. The sky is black and clear. He steals a glance at Charles. He wants to say you did see it. He wants to say there's no way anybody could have missed it. He wants to say the factory has been chosen, that the big man himself will be here soon, he is sure of it. He wants to say wasn't it beautiful. He wants to say we are not alone. "You can really see the stars," he says, "when you get just a little outside the city."

Charles picks up his newspaper.

9

THEY ARE SITTING in the chairs, watching the Mexicans and the bearded men arrive to the field, where they drink fancy coffee and look at their phones. The head Mexican is wearing shorts again, this time with flashy red high tops. He gets out of the usual white Northwest Appalachian Energy truck and calls the bearded one over while the rest of them sleepily unload their strange tools and instruments. The Mexican has a large keyring on his belt and he uses it to unlock the storage boxes they have left behind.

They are far enough away that Howard can hear them talking but he cannot hear what they are saying. He is positive the things they are saying would only serve to annoy him, or make him feel small and left out, or even worse maybe they are meandering around this beautiful American field getting paid in real American dollars to speak Mexican, and so he has come to regard this situation as optimal.

The Mexican has given them no instructions so they just wander around, unloading this, taking out that, looking at their phones and sipping at their white coffee cups. The Mexican is no supervisor of men, that Howard is sure about. The job itself is likely some kind of hand out, some Democrat scheme to take good money and give it away to all the wrong kinds of people. He wonders what Mr. Tom Williams would think if he were to survey the work style at Northwest Appalachian Energy.

If Mr. Tom Williams walked down that hill with his square jaw and salt and pepper hair, his linebacker arms and Pitt degree and soft Ohio drawl, his Korean service and a brand new Ford F-150 every single year, these kinds of men would just stare at their phones, or ask him for a hand out, or look to the Mexican to fix everything in his fussy way.

"Remember Mr. Williams," he says.

Charles moves the newspaper. "Certainly," he says.

"A good man," Howard says. He wants to say what happened to men like that? What happened to respect? What happened to us? His throat wells.

"Think he wound up…I want to say Alcoa? When everything here went, you know."

Alcoa. Of course, Mr. Tom Williams would wind up at one of the big ones. "Is that aluminum?" he says. "Insurance?"

"It's Alcoa," Charles says.

"Hey guys."

Howard jumps.

"What can we do you for?" Charles says.

The Mexican is standing right there in front of them. He is younger than Howard had thought. He is jangling his key ring. He looks annoyed and a little nervous and Howard notes that they may be old but at least they can still make this kind of man a little nervous. Not everything is lost. Not anymore.

"We had an instrument in one of those lockboxes, down at the site?"

"Okay," Charles says. Howard is annoyed that Charles seems to have taken on the role as their leader and spokesperson.

"You didn't see anything last night, did you?" the Mexican says. "Anybody nosing around any of our stuff down there."

"I didn't realize I was your security guard," Charles says.

"Look —" the Mexican starts.

"But no, nobody was rummaging around in your precious lockbox."

"It's a pretty expensive instrument," the Mexican says and his tone has changed from nervous to angry, accusatory. He is looking around the little encampment. He walks over and picks up a jacket Howard has left on the ground. He looks at the powerbars, the bag where they put the wrappers, the thin blankets sitting on the dirty ground.

"Was your box still locked?" Charles says.

"What?"

"Your lockbox. Was it indeed locked?"

The Mexican takes out his phone. He starts tapping.

"Stay out of our shit," he says.

10

HOWARD WAITS UNTIL he is sure Charles is asleep and when he hears the slurping snores he gets up out of the chair, gestures toward the field, whispers "I'm just going to…" and moves out of the parking lot over toward the border. The night is quiet but for the gravel snapping beneath his feet, the insects' high whine, a white noise he has gotten quite used to and is unsure if he could sleep without. He pauses at the ridge where the parking lots gives way to the field. Or, what used to be the field and is now a series of gravelly foundations and strange machinery. A grid.

He doublechecks to make sure that Charles has not moved, that he is truly sleeping and not just waiting to catch Howard doing…whatever it is he is doing. He is only walking. Just a man on a walk late at night, clearing his lungs, getting some exercise. It could even be regarded as security, what he is doing, and he is well aware of how important security is to the factory, the nation, the big man himself. If they had monitored her emails the way Howard monitors the factory, the road, the border, even the field where the Mexicans have made their strange grid, where they stand around drinking their fancy coffee and staring at their phones, maybe the country would never have gotten to these dire circumstances.

He wonders if they have cameras, drones, if the chemtrails are communicating with the cloud to send images right now, Charles asleep with his Steelers cap pulled tight over his eyes and ears while Howard patrols the area. Even the Mexicans at Northwest Appalachian Energy would likely appreciate the service, making sure their grid is intact, their strange machines and piles of gravel, rock, and sand.

He calls for Mavis: cheep, cheep, cheep-cheep. He pauses at the border and then continues on past the strange machines. He examines the lockboxes, now secured by two locks each and bound together with some kind of industrial strength metal coil. He undoes his belt, pushes his pants down. He pulls them back up and looks toward the road to ensure that Charles is not standing there in judgement. He urinates on the lock boxes, a gentle stream that stops and starts. He used to hear about this, mostly jokes from old comedians, references on Sanford and Son or Barney Miller, and he thought how ridiculous it sounded. Trouble urinating? And then all of the sudden he was having trouble urinating and there was not a single thing funny about it. He wonders if he could talk to Charles about this, but then he flashes on Charles making some snide remark and puts the idea out of his head. Best to not put any extra arrows in that quill.

He anticipates tomorrow morning, standing on the border while the main Mexican or the Bearded One fumbles with the locks, the chains, wipes his hands on his face, in his beard, his shorts. One time last week he saw the Mexican go from unlocking the boxes to handling a breakfast sandwich and he wanted to call out to Charles, to shake hands, proclaim this small victory in the battle to make it great again. He has already decided that he will tell the men who are in charge what he has been doing, that they will consider it a significant if silent victory over the Mexican and Northwest Appalachian Energy and whatever it is they are doing here. By that time he imagines their equipment will be gone, the grid erased, their rock and sand and gravel trucked back to wherever it came from. He wonders if they will give him a supervisory position – not Mr. Tom Williams himself's job but something on the line, something in middle management or security. He has certainly been distinguishing himself and if they do have cameras, drones, cloud information, they will already know that by the time they arrive.

Cheep cheep. Mavis. He freezes.

"Cheep cheep," he whispers. He looks back toward the road, over to where the Northwest Appalachian Mexicans like to look at their phones while the head Mexican unlocks things and clicks away at his computer. He sweeps the edge of the forest, already becoming littered with wrappers and cans and cigarettes. "Mavis," he whispers. There is a rustling along the right edge at the place where the little creek loops out toward the forest. Before Northwest Appalachian Energy showed up he had been considering fashioning some kind of fishing pole.

Cheep cheep. Click click. There right at the edge of the trees, her green head poking through the brush, nearly invisible in the twilight. She takes a step forward and he can see her full body now. She is beautiful and strange, nearly seven feet tall, small dinosaur arms and heavy legs, a tail that trails back into the brush, her sharp, intelligent head covered in light feathers. She looks at home in these woods, even as she takes another tentative steps toward him. She is alert, coiled, her eyes twitching back and forth between Howard and the construction site.

"Cheep cheep," he says, and she pauses.

Click. Click click click. She is making the noise deep in her throat.

"Mavis," Howard says. He realizes how long it has

been since he's talked to somebody other than Charles. He wonders if the State Farm guys have noticed his absence, if any postcards have come from Leah, if he could get the cell phone she gave him turned back on again, would it still have that text message and the picture of them at the Pirates game. "Mavis, I saw the most amazing thing yesterday," he whispers.

She bobs her head. Click click.

"But you probably saw it too," he says. "It was beautiful, wasn't it? Just beautiful. And the factory. When they..."

Click click. She bobs her head. She snaps it forward, almost like she is threatening him. Click click. She snaps her head forward again, takes another step in his direction.

"Mavis it was...I never..."

She pauses. They are standing twenty yards apart. He can see her coiled muscles, the sharp claws. She could leap and be on top of him before he even turned to run.

"Did you see it, Mavis?" he says.

She backs up a step. Click click.

"Oh no," he says. "No let's just talk here, you and me. Just you and me."

She takes a step back. Another.

"Cheep cheep," he says.

She nods her head. Click click click click click click! She turns and bursts back into the forest. Howard takes a few steps forward but all he sees is the edge of the woods and then clustery blackness.

He looks toward the parking lot. Charles is still sleeping, no doubt. His cough is getting worse. They will be here soon and when they arrive Howard will have a lot to tell them. He wonders what the big man would make of Mavis, but then by the time he gets here he would

42

know all the big secrets anyway, Roswell and chemtrails and the Zodiac and maybe they have even found her emails by now, maybe they knew where they were all along and kept quiet because it was in the best interest of the country. These people have not been quiet, not been in the best interest of the country, making gays marry and sending men like Charles and Howard and Mr. Tom Williams off to the sidelines with their tails dragging between their legs. He stares at the empty space where Mavis was just standing. Mavis is out there. The big man will be here soon. There are miracles in this world, he thinks, and finally he has put himself in exactly the right place to see them.

11

HOWARD WAKES WITH a pleasant feeling. He shifts in his chair, feels the ache in his knee, the cold on his face. Charles coughs his wet cough. It is still dark, grey. What was he dreaming about? A positive memory, a warm feeling. Some kind of animal. A pet. Mavis.

Leah's dog, a scrappy, intense little thing they called a mutt then and now he supposes they would call her a pitbull. Somehow all the dogs have become pitbulls, something he imagines will be changing soon. Howard remembers golden retrievers and great danes, beagles and poodles and chocolate labs. Those were the great American dogs. Now these pitbulls are taking up all the space. There is some association with the rappers, he knows, those black fellows who say a song and don't even know how to play any instruments, who use words he is forbidden to use, was forbidden to use, words they used to use as much as they wanted to around the factory as long as Richardson or Smart was out of earshot.

He is losing the pleasant feeling. Best to focus on the future, on making it great again here at the factory. Those rappers with their pitbulls and their chains and n-words had their day and that day is done.

He always did have a soft spot in his heart for Mavis, though, mostly because of the way Leah looked at her, talked to her, the patience she showed for a young woman. It all seemed like a good sign, like good parenting had been happening, like Leah was going to be able to write her own ticket, do whatever she wanted to do.

He stands and stretches. If he is being honest, the problem is that she did that exact thing.

Charles shifts in his chair. The sun is rising. Howard has always been good at estimating time and he guesses it to be around six thirty. Charles has been sleeping later, going to sleep earlier, taking long naps in the afternoon while the Northwest Appalachian Mexicans pack up their things and look at their phones. Howard is not sure how the men in charge will view Charles when they arrive, if their cameras and drones and clouds will reveal him to be less a worker than perhaps they remembered. Howard has distinguished himself, of this he is sure.

Just then he has a thought: what if they find out about Leah? He has considered telling Charles, of course, considered telling Charles anything and everything about himself about a thousand times as they waited for their turn to arrive again. He has considered and carefully chosen to keep this one thing quiet. They have talked about their adult children but only in the most general terms: San Francisco, a registered nurse, no children.

Charles had been equally generic: the boy in Louisville and the girl all the way out in the Upper Peninsula of Michigan. Like Canada up there, he said. You can see the Northern Lights.

Howard had nodded and changed the subject so he would not have to admit that he had never so much as visited San Francisco, that the move had reduced Leah to phone calls and then texts and then the texts started coming late at night, very late for her, and they were mostly about the big man, about how could you vote for that person when you know that your daughter is a… he forces the word out of his head. An ugly word for an ugly thing.

Love is love, they say. Love is a text message with nothing but a link to a story in the fake news Washington

45

Post, sent at three forty-five in the morning, San Francisco time?

He realizes he is breathing heavily. Charles coughs and then spits. The first of the Northwest Appalachian Energy trucks moves down the road. It will be the shorts-wearing Mexican, Howard supposes. He does not understand the kind of man who would work every day in shorts, especially at whatever kind of outdoor job they are doing in the field. He does not understand the rest of them, meandering around and looking at their phones while the Mexican talks to the bearded one or shouts into his own phone, taps things onto his computer.

He flashes on his supervisor at Target. That job lasted a little longer than the others, before they did something to make him feel uncomfortable, before they ruined it for him again. This time they gave him that supervisor, a young Chinese named Tuvinh, with tattoos up and down each arm, a big rainbow flag right there on her forearm. And this person is supposed to be supervising the home section, telling Howard how to stock the bathroom amenities, how to fold a towel, cut open a box of queen linens?

A sound, wheels on the road. Charles stirs. This is not the Northwest Appalachian Energy truck, which puts lazily down the road. This sound is louder, aggressive, like a small steam engine pushing itself along. Charles opens his eyes and spits again. Howard notes that the consistency is decidedly gloppy, the blood to phlegm ratio roughly even. Howard stands and watches the pickup truck with the giant wheels returning again, making a turn in the parking lot before it pauses and the driver's side window comes down. The boy with the yellow pompadour nods to him, like last time, and then the window goes back up. Howard wonders how the boy gets in and out of the truck with those gigantic wheels. Does he jump? Or use some kind of rope to lever himself onto the wheels, where he may be able to push himself up onto the driver's seat. Is there a kind of lift system?

"What's this there then?" Charles says. His displeasure is plain.

"That same truck. From the other day," Howard says.

"The sam hill?" Charles says. "See anything else over there?"

"No," Howard says, and worries that he has answered too quickly. He pictures Mavis retreating back into the forest. A bob of her head, a click click and she was gone. He pictures the flying saucer, so beautiful, baptizing the factory. "Nothing but the usual," he adds.

Charles gives him a look. The truck moves over to where the Mexican will soon park his own truck. Howard is nervous and unsure why. This is a crack, a fracture in their careful routine, and not the one that they have been waiting for, of this he is sure.

The boy gets out of the car and surveys the place where the Mexicans have spray painted their grid. He places his hand over his eyes like an explorer surveying the land he will soon conquer. He is wearing khakis and a white dress shirt. He takes out his phone and takes several pictures, spanning the workspace, then he gets into his truck and leaves.

"What the..." Charles says.

"Something you think we have to...I mean..." Howard says.

"Just some kid," Charles says. "When they show up we can..."

"That's what I was thinking," Howard says.

Charles picks up his newspaper.

The truck pumps black soot into the air and Howard stares at the retreating cloud. Was that a feature the truck came with? Do all the new trucks do this now? Mr. Tom Williams' drove a pretty big truck but it was nothing in comparison to this boy's vehicle.

Howard sits and stretches. Right now the State Farm guys would be just getting there, settling in to their usual table, arguing about the Steelers and Penn State football, about who was going to pay the tab or something about corporate. When they reopen the factory, will they have a corporate? He had heard differing things about why they had to shut down in the first place, whether it would have helped to be bigger or these jobs were just going to China anyway and there was nothing anybody could do about it.

The Target manager wanted to talk about their feelings, about Howard's feelings, kept insisting how angry he was, asking why he couldn't just let things go and give her a chance. Let's just start fresh, she would say. Me and you, we can do this. She said it nice but he understood what she was saying, understood it without anything having to be said. Walk in the room with that kind of tattoo on your arm, with that many earrings and that short haircut and boots and you do not have to actually say a thing. It has all been said.

He wonders if they will go out after their first night, where they would go. Stoney's is gone. Dan's Café burned years ago. The Tavern or the Fireside or the Brickskeller may still be there. Or they may be some kind of a brewery now, a cidery or a winery or a distillery or more likely, a Starbucks. He likes a nice beer every now and then but none of this new stuff, everything so complicated and putting on airs. A beer should be a beer. The big man doesn't drink beer but Howard imagines that he is the kind of man who needs to stay on his toes. There are people looking to take him down, foreign operatives and porn stars and lawyers and Democrats and pizza parlor owners running kiddie porn rings right out of their basements.

What Leah has done is nothing like that, of course, but still he could never tell them, the men in charge. He could never tell the big man or Charles or Mr. Tom Williams. She used to show so much promise, with her math and her spelling. One Halloween she went as a vending machine, even dispensed candy if you dropped a coin into the slot on her shoulder, and Howard still believes it was possibly the most clever thing he had ever seen another person do. She used to call him Daddy, then Dad, then Howard, and then she stopped calling altogether.

The woman from Target used to call him Mr. Collins but he knew she was never serious about it, respectful. How can you be respectful when you are walking around like that?

The warm feeling from the dream is all gone now. He stands and watches the Northwest Appalachian Energy trucks begin their slow crawl in to their work space. The boy with the truck has only been gone five minutes and the field seems like a crime scene, like it has been altered somehow. Howard knows something the Mexicans don't and as he watches them milling about, sipping at their Starbucks and looking at their phones, he finds that he likes it. He likes finally being in on the joke, being in the majority again like they should have been all along. He likes watching people like the Target manager clasp their tattooed hands together and worry over the big man, over what it will mean when they make it great again, when men like him and Charles and Mr. Tom Williams take their rightful place again.

The Mexicans and the addicts stand right there next to one another and don't even say a thing. Howard wonders if there are any of those text messages from Leah. When he gets back from his first shift he will plug it back in, see if she has come to her senses.

Charles coughs, spits a globule of snot and blood onto the ground.

"I believe I'm going to…" Howard says.

"Do what you have to do," Charles says.

12

WHEN THEY TAKE their lunch break the Mexican in the shorts walks slowly up the hill, looking at his phone the entire time. Howard has been noting how little difference there is between when they are working and when they are taking a break. The only way he can tell is the Mexican shouts "break" when they are taking a break to look at their phones and wander around, and then they sit down or lay on their backs to look at their phones, which they hold in front of their faces like binoculars.

"Hey guys," the Mexican says. His Pittsburgh accent is as thick as Old Snyder's and Howard has a pang of guilt that he did not go to his former supervisor's funeral. "Yinz are...camping here or something?"

"Camping?" Charles says. "Really?"

"I mean I don't see no tents or nothing," the Mexican says.

"Don't see no tents or nothing," Charles says back.

"Yeah, so...none of my business I guess but soon the derricks are going to come up down there on the job and, I mean..." he pauses, looks at his phone. "I mean, shit, look corporate don't want me to be saying this to anybody but I say it anyway, okay, I mean, I'm trying to do the right thing here."

Charles snorts and then coughs. He spits to the side where, Howard notes, the Mexican can't see the blood, can't get concerned, tell Charles he should see a doctor, go to the emergency room, take up yoga or get himself a therapy dog or a community garden plot.

"Look I'm trying to be a good person here so I gotta tell you when those derricks go up and they start in with it, this ain't going to be a good place to be."

Derricks? Howard thinks. He is struggling to catch up, his brain forming an oil rig, then something from a television show, oil bubbling up out of the ground. Bubbling crude.

"Thank you but no thank you," Charles says. He leans over to spit.

"You should see somebody about that," the Mexican says. "Okay I said my piece."

"Beaners," Charles says low, so the man cannot hear. "We'll see what happens when the rest of them show up but I don't think it's going to go too well for the wetbacks down there."

Howard watches the man walk back down to the field. Derricks?

"I say not going to go very well for those…spicks and ingrates down there," Charles says.

It ain't going to be a good place to be. Mavis lives somewhere in those woods. But she has lived, he wonders how long? Centuries. The factory has been anointed.

"Suspect that's right," Howard says. He looks at the ground and then at Charles, who holds his gaze for a few seconds past when he would usually pull up the newspaper.

"Well I guess I better…" Howard says.

He waits for Charles to come back with the usual "do what you have to do" but all he gets is a curt page turn. Charles coughs something onto the parking lot, hacks and hacks and finally sits back up straight.

Howard wishes he had gotten up and wandered over to the check on Factory Right while all the coughing was going on. Now he will need to either say it again or just get up and leave, and neither seems like the best solution.

"Do what you have to do," Charles says finally, his voice is thin and for the first time Howard wonders if he is getting really sick. He stands, nods, and walks over toward the factory.

13

HOWARD POKES AT the hole in his boot. The left arm of his shirt is starting to come loose. He has tightened his belt twice and is down to the last notch. The thought peeks into his mind and he puts it away. No. It will not do. What if they never come back, if the factory never opens, what then? That is the kind of weak thinking that leads to weakness, factories shuttered, good men filling out a paper application at Target while Mexicans and blacks fill up their carts with televisions and standing fans and video games and movies and frozen empenadas.

The factories are going to open up again. Good jobs will come back. He heard the big man say it himself, in person. "We're going to bring back your coal industry, your steel industry. We're bringing it back," he said.

Howard had been standing near the entrance and if he is being honest, he was there mostly because the convention center was near the Lowe's and he needed some things. He was curious but was also pretty sure he would wind up voting for another one of the Bushes, who had been fine presidents, one of them even wore a flight suit and said mission accomplished and threw out the first pitch at a baseball game after 9-11. He hadn't really been following along too much other than just to be relieved that the black would no longer be the king of the free world. He knew that Leah hated the big man and wasn't sure what to do with that, so he had stayed out of it more or less.

But there, in that hall, among all the other left behind men and their wives, their sons and daughters, all of them wearing those red hats and shaking their fists, shouting and laughing and stoking the big man's fires as he really got going, chanting Lock Her Up and Drain the Swamp, he found himself feeling alive again for the first time in a very long time. His heart was beating. He was sucking the air. The big man said Pittsburgh is Steel City and when I'm president steel is coming back and they cheered, they hugged and laughed and shook hands and high fived and Howard was right there in the middle of it, the middle, Howard, the beating heart of Pittsburgh is steel city and when I'm president steel is coming back. He pushed into the crowd and nobody ignored him, pushed back, told him the ground was not his for the taking. He pushed into the crowd and the crowd absorbed him, welcomed him, swallowed him in to their fist shaking embrace. The big man said we're gonna build that wall and Howard chanted Build The Wall and a hundred thousand chanted along. The big man said her emails and Howard chanted Lock Her Up and it was glorious, that feeling of finally being able to say what had been building up in him, what had been clogging him up, pushing him into the shadows and the background, disappearing him one moment at a time. He had become so invisible, so grey, afraid to even whisper the things he was thinking, the things he knew, the things that were so obvious all along. They chanted Build That Wall and Lock Her Up but they really could have been chanting you were right, Howard. You. Were. Right. You, the one who they have been trying to make disappear, you were right all along. Everything you've been feeling, all of the isolation and confusion and repression. You were right. Everything you felt, every slight and insult and creeping disrespect, it was all right.

And it felt so good to do it right there in the open again, with a hundred thousand people all feeling the same way. You were right. Three hundred thousand of them shouting we were right. They were right, all two million of them. It was electric, as close as he had ever been to being a part of a mob and if all twelve million of them had marched out of that hall and down to Washington, DC to drain the swamp that very day he would have gladly joined. He would have drained that swamp. He would have built that wall. He would have locked her up. He would have done whatever it was that needed doing.

Now he stretches and listens to Charles cough. They will open the factory. "We're going to bring back your coal industry, your steel industry. We're bringing it back. Remember that, we're bringing it back, folks." Howard remembers. Howard remembers everything.

14

HOWARD IS JUST rounding the corner of the factory, almost done with his nightly excursion, when he hears the engine's huff. He looks to the sky, has been looking there for most of his walk, but it is cloudy and dark and there are no mysterious lights, no lights at all, much less a flying saucer. He pauses, registers the sound, and then realizes that it is the truck – not the quiet churn of Northwest Appalachian Energy but the low cycle of the boy and massive smoke belching supertruck. He wonders if he should wait there at the factory, let Charles take care of whatever the boy might want, but God and the big man move in mysterious ways and if they are watching he will want to be a part of this, whatever it is.

He continues along the factory wall, notes that the sneaker is still in the same place, the light that flickers sometimes is not flickering, the lights on the hill have turned on at their appointed time. All is well and in order. He imagines himself checking a column on a piece of paper. Factory Right Security Check: okay.

The truck is parked next to the camp chairs. As he gets closer Howard can see the window decal of the cartoon character urinating, the confederate flag in the cab window. The window decal is some cartoon character urinating on Hillary Clinton. Lock her up, he thinks. His heart races quickly when he thinks about the rally, shouting and pumping his fist and strangers just shaking his hand, high fiving, fist bumping, welcoming him into their happy angry midst.

"Oh there he is," Charles says. He is standing next to the boy. "This is Howard. Howard, this is…"

"B-rad," the boy says.

The boy is tall, with blond hair that is shorn thin on the sides and pompadoured on the top. It gleams with some kind of product, stays still when the boy walks over and shakes his hand. Strong shake.

"B-rad?"

"Like Brad but I say B-rad," the kid says. "It's my Twitter handle, Insta, you know. It's my YouTube. You might have seen some of it, under B-rad America."

Howard feels the surge briefly, that feeling that somebody is using some coded language to keep him out. For so many years he felt bad about this, felt that it was a problem with him, that he had done something to merit being shunted aside in this way, replaced by Mexicans and tattooed lesbians. But the big man started talking and Howard realized that it was unfair, all of it was unfair, that he did deserve the things he deserved and finally they were going to make the country great enough to give them back.

"What's the story with that vehicle?" Charles says. Howard notes that his tone, always so snarky, always with the implication that Howard is doing something wrong or not quite right, has turned ingratiating.

"That's my truck," B-rad says. "Pretty fucking nice huh?"

"I guarantee it," Charles says.

"How do you get in and out of it, wheels that size?" Howard says.

"So what are you guys doing here?" B-rad says.

"Waiting," Charles says.

"Like for a concert or something?"

"Waiting to get back what we deserve," Howard says. "Jobs. The factory."

"For real?" B-rad says.

"Expect any day now," Charles says. "Lot of activity lately."

"That factory?" B-rad says. "You're gonna work there?"

"I expect," Charles says.

B-rad pauses, staring at the factory. Howard realizes he is holding his breath, waiting for some kind of validation. The boy's hair is really remarkable, he thinks, the way it swoops up into a giant wave and then crests back, the way it never moves, the way it seems cemented into place with some kind of liquid. They have never really talked about what they are doing here at the factory. Howard wonders what the boy will think, if he is capable of breaking the fragile thread that has grown up around the two men and the camp chairs and the factory.

"You know they got all kind of wetbacks working down there at the frack thing," he says.

"Come again?" Charles says.

B-rad points to the field, the piles of gravel and the grid that has been laid out on the grass. "Appalachian? Fucking shitass company."

"They do got a bunch of Mexicans down there," Howard says.

"Right? Fire a fucking hard working white man and hire a bunch of fucking Mexicans."

"I take it you are the offended party?" Charles says.

"I who what now?"

"Got fired?"

"Out at Mohegan. They made up a bunch of bullshit about being late but you and I know what it was about."

"Damn straight," Charles says.

Howard feels the pull, a light echo of what he felt at the rally, shouting Lock Her Up and Build That Wall.

It is thrilling, talking about it all, finally, out here in the open. Just saying it. "It isn't right," he says.

"I guarantee it," Charles says.

"I think we need to do something about it," B-rad says. "Right here, right now."

15

THEY FOLLOW B-RAD down to the field. His shirt is starched white and Howard can still see where the creases were from the box. "You guys on YouTube?" he says. "I guess you're not or you might recognize me. Or maybe somebody sent you the one last month that went kind of viral? Thing about the gooks and the phones? The one where I started out like I was that Long Duck Dong guy from that movie? Never mind." They are moving past the place where they park their trucks, where they look at their phones and wander around. B-rad feels in his pocket and comes out with a key. "Dumbfucks never change these keys," he says. He opens one lockbox after another. Then he goes back to the first one and takes out a crowbar. He takes out another and hands it to Charles, who hands it to Howard. It feels like a ritual, like church or Boy Scouts or the halftime of a football game.

B-rad moves to the end of the lockbox and grabs the top edge with his crowbar, indicating for Howard to do the same on the other end. The crowbar feels heavy, useful, like a perfect tool and a weapon and Howard feels something he has not felt in a long time, since before the factory closed, maybe since high school football or those early days roaming around Lawrenceville looking for beer or trouble or girls or all of the above, twenty one and the world wide open for whatever he was going to do to it. He feels dangerous.

Charles has moved to the other side and checks the crowbars to ensure their purchase on the metal. He tugs, gives the thumbs up. "Three…two…" B-rad says. He looks to Howard and Howard nods. "One!" They pull while Charles pushes from the other side and the heavy container rolls, tips, empties its contents across the spray painted lines of the field. B-rad pulls a laptop, thick with some kind of shell, more a tool than a gadget, drops it on the ground. He moves over to the side and comes back with a sledgehammer. He takes a swing and brings the hammer down on the computer and there is a thick crack, the sound of glass, metal, the heavy thunk as the boy takes another swing at the machine. The boy stands and he is breathing heavily, wiping sweat from his brow with a white handkerchief. His hair is perfect but he checks it anyway, feeling the contours. "Hey guys," he says, and Howard notices a slight accent, neither Pittsburgh or Appalachia or exactly Midwest. He would guess somewhere in New Jersey. B-Rad puts the handkerchief across his face like an old fashioned bank robber. He takes out his phone and clicks on a few buttons and says "Hey guys. B-rad USA here where we're doing a little monkeywrenching on you know who out here giving jobs to, well, you know who." He pauses and wipes at something in his eye and his tone changes. "This is an invasion," he says. "We cannot allow these rats to invade our country. Our children are in danger. Children! We must immediately send these subhumans back from where they came. Our system is a mockery of what our white forefathers fought to defend. How do you stop these people, these caravans, these rats? You can't…I mean…shit," he pauses, takes off the handkerchief and checks something on his phone. "Neither of you is filming this?" he says. "I'm just…neither of you?"

Charles pretends to be checking his pockets. Howard is still trying to understand what is happening here, why the boy is talking to his phone, what they will do with the rest of the lockboxes. It had felt fantastic to be a part of a team again, part of the gears turning to make it great again. Charles holds up his hands. Howard taps the crowbar against his foot. When he thinks about it Charles did have kind of an easy role at the factory. When the men in charge come back, they will use their drones and their clouds and their wikileaks to find out who it was who toed the line here, who helped build this wall and who stood on the other side, pretending to push.

16

HOWARD WAKES TO the sound he has been expecting since they finally went to sleep last night, the truck chug chug chugging slowly out of the lot. He gauges the time. Six, six-thirty. The sky is dark gray. They have a few hours until the Mexican will come up the hill, maybe followed by the police or Nancy Pelosi herself. But no, he thinks. These are not the kind of people who take on their issues head on, not like Howard or Charles or Mr. Tom Williams, not like the big man or the people in charge now, the people in charge again, who have simply recognized that they deserved to be in charge and made it so. If they have videos on their drones and clouds they are surely having a high old time watching Howard and Charles and B-rad make their very own tea party with the property of Northwest Appalachian Energy.

He stands and stretches. Charles coughs and a long string of brown phlegm plops onto his jacket. Howard feels for a handkerchief, looks around the site for some kind of paper towel he could use to put his friend in a more dignified state. Are they friends, though? More like colleagues. Work friends. He stayed in touch with a few of the guys from the plant for awhile, a Steelers game every year with Old Snyder, beers at Harvey's every Thursday with Youndt, then every other Thursday, then once a month, and then Youndt's funeral at that sad little place outside Monroeville.

He wonders how big a company Northwest Appalachian Energy could even be. Until the Mexican and the beard drove up through the factory's own road and started painting the field, he had never heard of them at all. Do they even have a rightful claim on the field, with the factory so close and starting up again any day now? What did the Mexican mean when he said these places were not very nice to be around?

The worst thing about the Mexican, he thinks, is that yinzer accent he is putting on. The rest of it, the shorts and the greasy hair and the standing around looking at his phone when he is supposed to be leading men like Mr. Tom Williams, it is all annoying but predictable enough. It is almost not even his fault, he thinks. But that accent. It is clear to Howard now that with his dark skin and dark eyes and dark hair, his lazy way of shambling around, the way he tried to act like he was doing them a favor and then so quickly abandoned the whole thing, this Mexican is the same as the rest of them. No matter how many times he fakes a "yinz" he is part of the invasion B-rad was talking about. He is an invader.

B-rad kept on insisting he had "more than fifty thousand followers" and Howard understands that means something about the internet but he also knows somewhere in his gut that B-rad is not to be trusted. Not fully, the way one might trust Mr. Tom Williams or the big man. Howard remembers boys like B-rad in high school, soft rich kids who folded the first time an opposing linebacker tried to put a finger in their eye at the bottom of a pile, smart kids in their college sweatshirts afraid to acknowledge his presence at the Tavern when they were home for Thanksgiving break.

The boy did make some things happen, though, that is for sure. Everything from the Northwest Appalachian Energy lock boxes is either smashed or lined up along the border to the parking lot. "Build that wall!" they chanted as they piled up the broken bits of laptops and other strange equipment that looked like it would be used for some kind of monitoring or drilling.

"See this?" B-rad would call as he pulled another strange device out of the lock box. "Thirteen thousand dollars." And then he would smash it with the sledgehammer or toss it to Howard to hit like a baseball.

Howard wonders exactly how much damage they did last night. He chuckles. Sorry snowflake, he thinks. We are back in charge now. He stands, whispers, "I'm just gonna…" and Charles coughs his sleepy assent.

He walks down to where they have assembled all the pieces of the broken things from Northwest Appalachian Energy. Today it looks more like some mounds than a wall. "Build that wall!" they had shouted. They had high fived, giggled, hugged. B-rad smelled like expensive laundry detergent and cotton candy.

He wonders if it is too late to put the things back together, throw them away, move them deep into the woods where nobody will ever find them. He wonders if Mavis was watching them last night, bobbing her head and clicking as they shouted "Lock her up!" and "Fuck Hillary!" He is glad that he fought the urge to tell Charles and B-rad about Mavis. He is not sure why but he is sure that it would be best to keep Mavis a secret. It is the same feeling he has about Leah, about what she is, who she lives with, what she does in private. It would be nice to talk about it with somebody but it would also be information that could be used against him in any future interactions. Charles has his ways. Charles with that information would not be a wise move.

Howard will wait until the new men in charge show up and only then will he tell them exactly what they have hiding in their woods. Something twitches along the tree line and Howard takes a step in that direction. Cheep-cheep, he calls. A deer emerges from the woods, a buck, ten points at least, moving strong and smooth. Cheep-cheep, Howard calls, and it freezes, its nose twitches, and it explodes back into the woods.

He is doing it again, ruining everything.

No, he reminds himself. Not anymore. Lock her up. Build that wall. He will need to be the person he was at the rally, unafraid and ready to re-take what is and always was rightfully his. They will repel the invaders and the factory will open and Leah will tell him it was all a big reaction, that she had read too many books and watched too much MSNBC, listened to too many of those rap records, and she would be coming home to find a nice boy to settle down with, maybe have a few linebackers of her own for Howard to bounce on his knee.

The forest is still, the sky just starting to lighten. Everything is green and gray, trees starting to take shape in his vision as the sun rises. There is a faint buzzing that gets louder until he can see it, the UFO, zeppelin-shaped and gray. In the rising morning he can tell that it is scraped up and dirty and looks more like an instrument of war, a tank or a jeep that has seen some action, than a shiny spaceship. The zeppelin moves smoothly across the parking lot and pauses over the field. A light strafes the area where they have made their wall.

Howard is frozen but he is not afraid. It is all happening. He wishes again that he had brought the cell phone, or one of those disposable cameras. He wonders if Charles is watching but he does not see anything at the site but the empty chair and Charles reclined and likely still asleep. If B-rad was here they would get the word out to his fifty-thousand followers and they would be famous, the factory would be famous and they would have to hurry up and send the new men in charge to open up as soon as possible. The big man likes pomp, he likes circumstance. He likes reality television shows and Playboy bunnies and paying women to keep their pretty mouths shut after he grabs them right in their you know whats. The big man is a big character and nothing is bigger than this.

The zeppelin lights suddenly pulse and the entire field is bathed in neon green and then Howard hears a low zap and sizzle and the machine shoots straight up and it is gone and so is all the Northwest Appalachian Energy equipment, left in their place a series of burn marks on the grass, a tight spiral that looks distinctly like something a spaceship might leave after it vaporized a pile of broken materials.

Howard realizes he is sitting down. He does not remember doing this but his legs are weak, his fingers tingling, his breath is shallow. The hum remains in his head and he is still surprised to see the dark hole where the spaceship just was. He should stand. He should talk to Charles. He should see if they are here yet, the head men in charge. He has a feeling that they will be here very soon, that one minute they will not be here and the next they will, all of them, filing in to do their good American jobs, clapping each other on the back, making jokes, making plans for a few pops after work.

The sun is coming up and the forest has turned from grey to green and brown. The burn marks are noticeable but there is nothing else on the field. No spray paint, no empty lockboxes, nothing but grass and six spirals. He thinks of those crop circles he has seen on the television. He wonders if the aliens may be talking to the big man through the chemtrails, if he has been chosen to witness all of this for Mr. Tom Williams or whoever the new men in charge will be. They may be watching right now with their clouds and drones and he looks up into the lightening sky and holds his thumb up to let them know that he knows. He knows and he likes it. He knows and he will continue to take care of things here on the ground with the Mexican and the bearded one and the rest of the ingrates. He knows and they have chosen the right person to be in charge until the other men can get here.

17

CHARLES IS ON his knees, vomiting a brown and bloody puddle onto the parking lot when Howard gets back. He looks small, too thin, a scarecrow of a man in a cartoonishly large flannel shirt and dungarees. At the place where his work coat rides up, Howard can see the clear outline of his spine. How long have they been out here? Howard has lost track of the days, weeks, months. It is cold enough to be November but it also could be March.

Charles finishes with a series of coughs and gurgles and returns to his camp chair, wiping at his mouth. Howard decides he will keep it all to himself, save it all for the new men in charge, for the big man and the white haired fellow and the brassy blonde lady who he knows must make Leah and all the rest of the lesbians and punkers and blacks and Democrats so angry.

"Expect they'll be up here to see us soon," Charles says.

"Build that wall," Howard says.

"Are they…" Charles says.

"I don't know," Howard says, and feels guilty in the lie but more assured than ever that he needs to save it all for the right moment. "I just did Factory Left. All ship shape over there. That one sneaker is really looking worse for the wear lately, but…"

"Is he…" Charles says.

"Left earlier," he says.

"Interesting boy."

"Sure got us stirred up, didn't he?"

"Gonna be real interesting when your Mexican friend shows up today."

Howard wants to tell him everything, that he has seen the most amazing things at the factory, a dinosaur and a UFO and a house on the hill where a good American just like him, just like them, turns the lights on every night at 7:45 on the dot. He wants to tell him that they were right about everything, that the factory has been blessed from the skies, anointed, that the big man is watching from the cloud and the wikileaks, that he has seen proof with his very own eyes just a few minutes ago, that the big man has access to the most amazing things and he is already using them to drain the swamp, lock her up, build that wall, make America great again.

"Gonna be real interesting," he says.

"Was kind of hoping the boy would be here for that part," Charles says. "Some muscle, know what I mean?"

"Oh I don't think we'll need that," Howard says. "They wouldn't dare. Not now. Not anymore."

Charles coughs and coughs.

"Are you…" Howard says.

Charles waves him off, wipes his mouth with the sleeve of his work jacket. "Might could use a cough drop or two," he says. "Expect our little tea party last night will bring the factory people along sooner than later."

"I expect," Howard says. He feels elated, exuberant, like he could fly up into the sky. In the mix of all of it, a sudden pang of the old sadness: if Ginny was here. If he could get to a phone he might call Leah. He wonders if she would understand or is she so far gone she would just brush him off and complain about racism or sexism or the environment and other things he could care less about even when her own father, a good man, a solid

71

working man has witnessed an actual and true miracle, has seen with his own eyes what the big man can do with his power and his wikileaks. The last text he got from her was at something like four in the morning San Francisco time. I cannot believe you voted for that person.

Cars on the road. Howard stands. Charles shifts in his chair and Howard notes that he tries to stand but remains seated, seems to sink a little further into the camp chair. He is disappearing cell by cell, minute by minute, just like Howard has been for the past twenty years, one job application, welfare check, doctor's visit, unreturned phone call, Mexican getting a job, tattooed Lesbian supervisor at a time. No more.

The Northwest Appalachian Energy trucks arrive at their usual lazy pace. Doors open. Shouting. The Mexican talks to the bearded hipster while the rest of them mill around looking at their phones and drinking their five dollar coffees. The Mexican calls somebody on his phone, shouts into it, calls somebody else. He turns and looks at Howard, his hands on his hips, shaking his head in disbelief.

A long black SUV with no license tags rolls down the road. This is it. Howard imagines what it will be like when the big man gets out. Will he have the white-haired fellow with him or the attractive daughter? Maybe one of the handsome sons. Maybe he will bring Nancy Pelosi to show her how good hard-working Americans work before he locks her up, as well. The Mexican signals at the SUV but it continues up the driveway and stops near Howard's own Lincoln. Howard wishes he had brought the red baseball cap he had bought at the rally, $39.99, a good solid baseball cap, American manufacturing practices at work. But the big man already knows everything, has been watching and will certainly commend Howard for his good work at the factory.

"No sir," Howard imagines himself saying. "I do not want a cabinet position or even Mr. Tom Williams's job. I'll just be happy to go back to my old position on the line." Howard realizes he can't quite imagine what that work was like anymore. Did he use a die press, or punch holes in something? He was not a coal miner but is glad the big man is going to bring coal back, has probably already brought it back. Good American jobs. Did he inspect something or were they making steel? Forging steel. Very American good work. He just remembers that it used to be good, that he felt useful and part of something bigger and at the end of the day they would clap one another on the back and have the kind of respect that they just weren't giving out in America when the black was in charge but were now, are now, and now the big man would be stepping out of that big American SUV any minute to finally recognize all of it.

The driver's door and the passenger door swing open at the same time and a man and woman are walking toward him. They are attractive, thirtyish, both wearing sunglasses and dark suits. They look official but shouldn't they be opening the door for the big man? The man pulls a wallet out of his pocket and flashes a badge. FBI. "Agent Barnard and Syens. FBI," he says. The woman nods.

"Officer who what now?" Charles says.

"Agent Barnard," the man says. The woman taps her feet. She seems annoyed at all of them, disappointed to find herself in this particular parking lot on this particular day talking to these particular men. She looks behind them, watches the Mexican and his men shuffling around, talking on their phones, looking at their phones, sitting on the ground doing nothing with their phones sitting next to them, and then turns back to stare at her partner, who is talking about federal jurisdiction this and special operations that. Howard never did understand what was so difficult about staying at home, about making a home, tending to the children and looking pretty and smoking cigarettes and doing…whatever it was Ginny did while he was out at the factory with Charles and Mr. Tom Williams being hard-working Americans at their jobs doing…he is sure they did something important. They worked hard. They were hard-working Americans making a good wage. Hard-working Americans making a good wage with respect in the community, from the children, the teenagers, the women, and the blacks and the Mexicans knew enough to stay in their place, to respect the troops and the police and all the hard-working Americans who were doing their share, carrying the load, clocking in and clocking out and doing…whatever it was they did to make it great.

"Either of you see anything…unusual out here last night," the man says. He tips his sunglasses up on his nose, runs a hand through his shaggy hair. The man can't be more than 35. He is good looking, a slow talker whose shirt is hanging out the left side of his black pants. "Maybe four, five in the morning?"

"Unusual how?" Charles says. He puts his hands on the camp chair like he is going to stand, leans forward, and then thinks the better of it. Even in his reduced capacity there is something puckish about him, combative, and for once Howard is glad for Charles and his airs.

"We've had some reports in this area," the man says. "UFOs. Lights in the sky. Some kind of…"

"Unusual activity," the woman says. "Don't put words in their mouths."

"Unusual activity," the man says. He looks at the cars covered in dust, at the dark factory, the Mexicans and the ingrates staring at their phones at the field. His

74

eyes scan the treeline and Howard wills Mavis to keep her head on the other side of the trees for now. "Hey what are...are you guys living out here?"

"Living out here. That's rich," Charles says.

"What's that?" the woman says, pointing to the puddle of blood and phlegm and vomit off to Charles' side. "I'm a medical doctor," she adds. She walks over and leans down next to the puddle.

"Something didn't agree with me last night," Charles says.

"How long have you been out here? Exposure to the elements can cause extremely deleterious effects on the body," the woman says.

They hear music first, some kind of heavy guitars mixed with Irish sounds and a singer who is shouting something that Howard cannot ascertain. They see the smoke and hear the great roar of the engine as more black smoke pushes into the air. B-rad is back. He stops at the Northwest Appalachian Energy site, revs the engine, blasts more black smoke into the air. The Mexican waves a hand over his face and walks quickly to the treeline, shouting into his cell phone. B-rad continues up the slight hill and into the parking lot.

The FBI man takes in their reactions. "This is somebody you know," he says. It is not a question, just a comment, and Howard notes that the FBI agent may be smarter than he looks. "See that?" he says to his partner, nodding at the decals along the back and windows of the massive pickup.

B-rad swings down off the seat and runs a comb through his hair. "The fuck?" he shouts. He points at Howard. "You cleaned it all up, you pussy?"

"Hello!" the woman FBI agent says. She holds up a badge. "FBI."

"Fake news," B-rad says, brushing past her. "You got rid of it all. You pussied out," he says, looking at Howard first and then Charles.

The agent holds out her badge again. "FBI," she says. "We're going to need you to explain what you're talking about. Did you all see something last night?"

"Syens, let's…" the other agent says. He turns to B-rad. "Don't go anywhere. That's an order," he flashes his badge again. "You two as well," he says. Charles coughs. Howard nods. "We're going to go talk to these fellows, see what's going on here," he says.

Howard looks to the road for a line of black SUVs. Perhaps they will arrive in helicopters. Perhaps the UFO itself. He knows what he saw. He knows what it meant but even so he cannot calm the pang of unrest gurgling in his belly.

"The fuck you fuckers?" B-rad says. He jabs a finger on Howard's shoulder.

"Hey!" Howard says. He means it to come out as jokey, as we're all in this together, but the word sounds defensive and raw in his mouth. Who is this boy to be poking a hard working American man like Howard?

"The shit's gone and you two are the only ones out here," B-rad says.

"We don't…we didn't…" Charles says. He coughs once, twice, three four five six seven times and then leans over and hocks up a pink line of spit and phlegm.

"Dude this is awful the shit's not there then what's the point? I'm never going to be able to…I mean I can't…" he holds up his phone. "I can't even…"

Howard has been holding his tongue, keeping it all in for too long. He has stayed silent through being mocked and marginalized and replaced, through terrible interviews and lesbian supervisors who want to talk about his anger, through Mexicans taking all the jobs and her emails just going away like poof, through chemtrails in his beautiful blue sky and child pornography rings being run right out of pizza places. He will not hold his tongue anymore. Now is the time. He is among friends.

Is he among friends? Charles wipes his mouth on the sleeve of his work jacket. He must weigh seventy-five pounds. B-rad wears a tight tee shirt that says Proud Boys and a bandana around his neck. His khakis look expensive. That truck must be worth two hundred thousand dollars.

The FBI agents are still talking to the Mexican. "I saw something," Howard says. He checks to make sure the FBI agents are out of earshot. The bearded guy stands along the treeline, looking deep into the woods. Howard fights the urge to shout at him to back up, stay away from Mavis. The woman FBI wanders away and stares up at him. She scans the landscape. Something about it feels like a ticking clock. Something is going to happen and it is going to happen soon.

They are not paying attention to him, Charles sitting rigid with his eyes closed, B-rad typing something into his phone. "Hey," Howard says. "Hey! I saw something last night."

"He saw something," Charles says. He coughs and doesn't even bother to wipe his mouth. Cough cough cough. He grips the sides of the camp chair, leans forward, and then sinks back into the chair again. He waves a hand in a dismissive gesture and something in him recedes, he shrinks again. He is disappearing. It is coming faster.

"What are you talking about?" B-rad says, but his tone is annoyed and incurious.

Howard regards the two men. He checks the FBI agents, still talking with the Mexican. The bearded hipster is walking the treeline, his hand held up to his mouth like he is calling a dog.

"I saw something. Something in the sky. A zeppelin."

"Pshaw," Charles says.

"A UFO," Howard says.

"Dude," B-rad says. "Jesus Christ I mean I can't even with this," he looks at his phone again, swipes at his hair, which has not moved.

"You had to see it," Howard says, looking at Charles. "You had to hear it. It was right there. I saw it. It was real."

Charles leans over and vomits on the ground.

"Real," B-rad says. "Like that makes any fucking difference you old fuck. If I can't...if there's no...how am I supposed to live stream?"

"It was real," Howard says. He takes a step toward the boy. "I saw it with my own eyes."

"I don't care," B-rad says. "It makes no fucking difference. How am I going to…" he starts, and his face scrunches up. He sucks air. His mouth trembles. "Fuck it was going to be so perfect!" he says. Howard notices cars coming down the road, steady and slow, two police cars, three more Northwest Appalachian Energy trucks, two more black SUVs. He looks to the sky. Nothing. No helicopters or zeppelins. But there, off to the right, he sees it, a chemtrail, still staining the beautiful blue sky. So that is how they are watching.

"Don't you get it?" Howard says. "First time, it hovers right over the factory. Right over it, just humming up there, rattling with something, this big old zeppelin thing, antennae coming out of it, these markings, writing, signs or something. It looked like a flying tank, like a hundred tanks welded together and hovering over the

78

factory, our factory, hovering there in the dark and all of the sudden it's not dark anymore. It's not dark. It's light. It's light and that's when I knew. I knew that this was a sign. They were blessing us, acknowledging."

"Acknowledging what?" B-rad says. Charles remains still. His fists are clenched into balls and it seems like part of his right side has disappeared.

"That we're on the right path, we're here for the right reasons," Howard says.

"The fuck reasons?" the boy says.

"The factory. Here is where it all starts. Don't you see?" He wants to grab them, high five, shout Build that wall again. "Can't you see it? Don't you see that we've been chosen, the factory has been chosen and this is where it all starts. This is where we make it great again."

Down at the field, police are getting out of cars in their careful way, four more people stand around in black suits, a black and a Mexican and a woman and a regular man, by the looks of it.

"It's what I saw," Howard says. "This is real. It's all real. We were right. All along we were right."

"Real isn't…who the fuck cares? I can't fucking own the libs with a field full of nothing. You think that's going viral? They could be, I don't know, planning a fucking picnic down there. Divining for water or whatever you call it. Can't even get them pissed off about fracking with no fucking frack sites coming up. Motherfucker it was going to be perfect."

Charles tilts over further, his body splayed at a bad angle, legs pushing up against the right side of the chair. He chokes, coughs, tries to spit. He is shrinking, disappearing. His left hand is either balled into a fist or it has vaporized into thin air, like good American jobs, like hard-working men, like her emails, like Ginny and Leah and Mavis.

"Hey is he okay," the FBI agent says.

"What?" B-rad says. He fumbles with his phone.

The woman starts walking toward them. She is not bad looking, good looking actually. Ginny never would have put herself out here like this, standing in some UFO field with Mexicans and the FBI and their witch hunt. The FBI is leaning over Charles. His right arm is either tucked beneath his leg or it has disappeared altogether. "We're losing him," she says.

B-rad stands back, holding his camera up. He clicks a button and starts talking. "Hey guys," he says. "I'm here at the site of a...."

The FBI says something into a walkie talkie and the people on the field start running.

The FBI has Charles laid out on the ground and is administering CPR. Howard wonders if he should do something but he knows he has done everything right. He has read all the signals. He has built that wall. He has drained this swamp. He has done everything he could. He has been right all along.

The rest of the FBI agents rush up and make a circle around Charles and the woman. Two regulars, two women, a black, and a Mexican and this is the FBI?

Howard looks to the sky. He hears a whirr, a hum, a cheep cheep. It is Mavis. It is the UFO. It is the chemtrail talking to wikileaks, beaming his accomplishments back to the drained swamp in Washington, DC. It is Leah. It is Ginny. It is the big man himself. Drain that swamp. Build that wall. Lock her up.

The sound is getting louder and he lays down on his back, closes his eyes. Around him he can hear chatter, the agents shouting, B-rad narrating, the low hum of something in the sky. Is that Mavis cheep cheeping? The Mexican talking in his cell phone, the sound of the ingrates shuffling around the field staring at their phones and sipping five dollar coffees? Is that the factory, the industrial vroom of Good American Jobs, Mr. Tom Williams parking his Ford F-150, Old Snyder doing... what Old Snyder did, Youndt sweeping up his fingers and walking silently out of the factory floor, the respect in the eyes of Leah as he came through the door at ten on a Thursday night, fresh from a few post-work pops at the Tavern or Dietles?

The hum is getting louder and in the sky there is just the faintest dab of the chemtrail and he wonders if the big man can see him now, if he is standing in a situation room ordering these agents, even the women, the Mexican, the black, ordering them to do what they must to save this American hero, this hard working man, this man who did his time for the country right here at the factory and now, after so many dark years, is back to help us make it great again.

"Jesus now the other one is down," somebody says. B-rad chirps in the distance. The hum is getting louder. "How long were they out here? What were they doing?"

Howard feels hands on his chest. He tries to push them away but the hum is getting louder and he knows it must be the big man, coming on a helicopter, Air Force One, riding atop the zeppelin itself, coming to tell him they were right all along, all along they were right to take what was theirs, to work hard, to build walls and... whatever it was they built at the factory at those good American jobs, so hard-working and it was all so unfair for so long. Unfair. The humming has turned to a kind of vibration that starts in his head and expands all the way down through his fingertips. His eyes are closed but he can still see the sunlight and he waits for the zeppelin to blot it out. His hands are shaking, his feet feel like he has been walking around in the snow without boots. The sneaker, he thinks. He has not checked on the sneaker on Factory Left today. Last night it looked... different somehow, different in a way that he found hard to describe and then everything just went so...he wonders if he will ever see Leah again, if that text -- I cannot believe you voted for that person -- will be the last thing he ever hears from her.

"Can you hear me?" the woman FBI is saying. "Sir. Can you hear me?"

Can you hear me? Could they ever hear him? Did they want to, did they even try? Charles is gone, of that he is sure. Disappeared. Shriveled up to nothing, same as Howard at Target, Howard at Wal-Mart, Howard shuffling in to that rally with no idea of what to expect. He feels fingers on the buttons of his shirt, hands on his chest. Cheep cheep. He opens his eyes and there she is just for a second, Mavis standing there over him, her funny nose twitching, her intelligent eyes smiling at him. I see you, they say. We are the same.

He tries to sit up, holds a hand out to touch Mavis's green cheek.

"Okay sir," the female FBI says. Her voice is overly calm, like a schoolteacher or a waitress telling him he needs to leave or buy another cup of coffee. "Stay with us," she says. Hands at his neck. "We're losing him," she says.

Howard closes his eyes. He stretches, makes himself larger, like a cat about to enter a confrontation. He will not disappear. He will not fade away, blend into the background, ease into the shadows, not again. He is here. His time has come again. Soon the big man will show up in a blaze of helicopters and confetti and gold plated balloons, machine guns and zeppelins and giant pickup trucks gloriously spouting black exhaust up toward the blue skies laced with wikileaks, and they will all reap what they deserved all along. They will build that wall. They will drain that swamp. They will lock her up. They will make it great again.

Acknowledgments

This book is the place where I put a lot of my anger and confusion and incredulity over what's happened in the United States during and since the 2016 election. That's not a surprise to anybody who has made it this far in the book. Like most of you who made it this far, though, what's in this book is nowhere near the full scope of that anger, confusion, and incredulity. The rest of it was experienced in drips and drabs, comments and rants and weird emotions shooting off in bad directions by my wonderful partner, Lori Wieder, who weathered it all with good humor and common sense and understanding, despite carrying her own rightful doses of anger, confusion, and incredulity. Thank you, Lori. I cannot imagine living this life without you.

Thanks also to my *Barrelhouse* family, Becky Barnard, Christina Beasley, Dan Brady, Tara Campbell, Killian Czuba, Erin Fitzgerald, Joe Killiany, Chris Gonzalez, Mike Ingram, Tony Mancus, Tom McAllister, Susan Muaddi-Darraj, Matt Perez, and Sheila Squillante, for being my happy sane safe normal fun place now and for the past however many years. If I didn't have you I would be crazy and also a real pain in the ass.

Thanks to Jon Roemer for trusting me with another very strange little book. From you, I know that "It's a Housley" is an actual compliment, and for that I'm eternally grateful.

About the author

Dave Housley is the author of the novel *This Darkness Got to Give*, and four story collections, most recently *Massive Cleansing Fire*. His work has appeared in *Booth, Hobart, Quarterly West, Redivider*, and some other places. He's one of the Founding Editors and all around do-stuff people at *Barrelhouse*. He is the Director of Web Strategy at Penn State Outreach and Online Education. He tweets at @housleydave.